Pussy cat, pussy cat, where have you been?

I've been to London to visit the King.

Russell Punter

Illustrated by Dan Taylor

Pussy cat, pussy cat,
where have you been?

I've been to London
to visit the King.

Pussy cat, pussy cat,
what did you see?

I'll tell you the story,
just listen to me...

I sailed up the Thames,
where a chilly wind blew.

They raised Tower Bridge so that I could get through.

On the banks of the Thames
stands the Tower of London.
Once traitors were held in its dark dingy dungeon.

I met the Beefeaters, who work there today.
They guard the Crown Jewels – it's a sparkling display.

The Shard is a tower
with a breathtaking view.

I took in the sights
from floor seventy-two.

I strolled to the Globe
where I stood in the yard,
for a play by Will Shakespeare. Some call him the Bard.

At Saint Paul's Cathedral,
I had fun with sound.

In the dome, if you whisper...

...you're heard all around.

If you don't want to walk,
you can hop on a bus.

One whizzed me through London without any fuss.

In Trafalgar Square,
where tourists rush by,
a statue of Nelson looks down from on high.

He fought in sea battles
a long time ago.
Four mighty bronze lions sit proudly below.

The next thing to try
was the huge London Eye.

It's a wheel that can take you
far up to the sky.

You stand in a capsule.
The wheel turns around.

You can see the whole city,
spread out on the ground.

On Westminster Bridge,
I went for a ride,
to the Houses of Parliament on the far side.

Big Ben is a bell.
It chimes on the hour,
from the belfry inside the Elizabeth Tower.

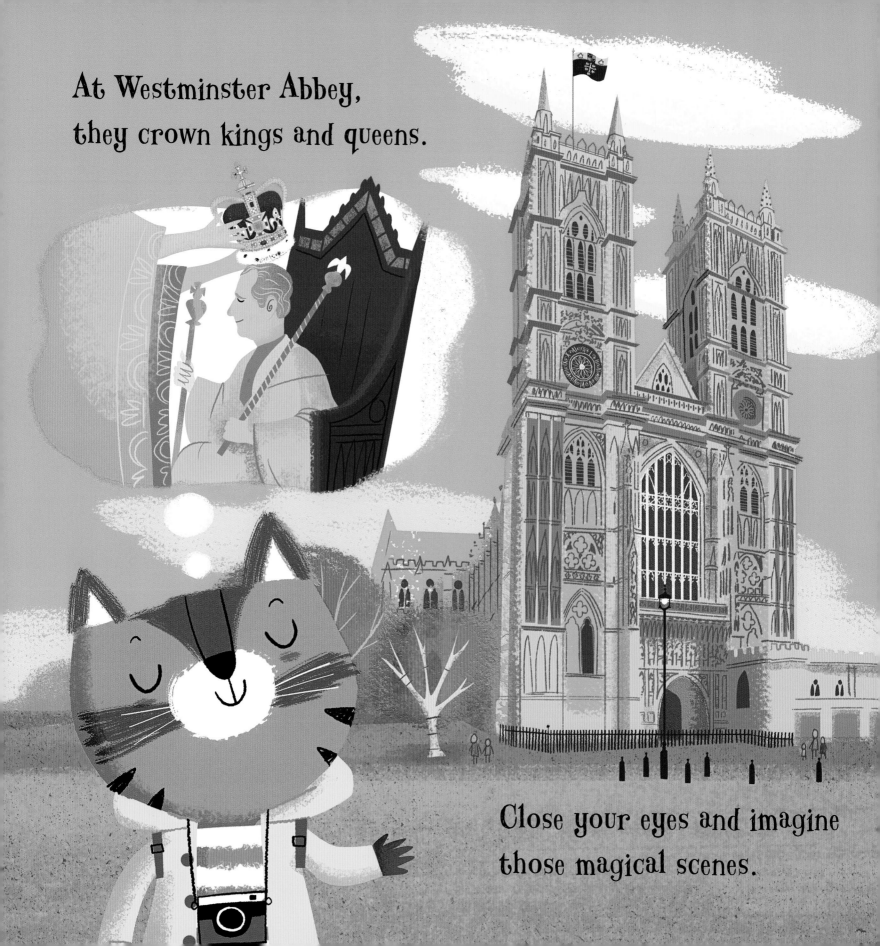

At Westminster Abbey,
they crown kings and queens.

Close your eyes and imagine
those magical scenes.

I took a black cab
to the Royal Albert Hall,

where a wild-haired conductor
was having a ball.

At Buckingham Palace
the guardsmen marched past.
I'd saved the best part of my journey 'til last.

The King's Guard paraded.
Their band played with pride.
When the marching had finished, I strode on inside.

I saw royal paintings...

...the grand dining room.

I was sure I would talk to His Majesty soon.

When I got to the place
where he sits on the throne,
I was shocked to discover... he wasn't at home!

What a pity, dear kitty,
you went all that way...

But London is fun,
so I had a great day.

Edited by Lesley Sims

This edition first published in 2023 by Usborne Publishing Limited, 83-85 Saffron Hill, London EC1N 8RT, United Kingdom.
usborne.com Copyright @ 2023, 2015 Usborne Publishing Limited. The name Usborne and the Balloon logo are registered trade marks of
Usborne Publishing Limited. All rights reserved. No part of this publication may be reproduced, stored in a retrieval system or transmitted in any
form or by any means without prior permission of the publisher. UKE.